Suzie Bitner Was Afraid of the Drain

Suzie Bitner was afraid of the Drain

Poems & Illustrations
by

BARBARA R. VANCE

Suzie Bitner Was Afraid of the Drain

Copyright © 2010 Barbara R. Vance

COPPERPLATE PUBLISHING

PO Box 260503, Plano, Texas 75026-0503

www.suziebitner.com

•

First Copperplate Publishing hardcover edition April 2010

ISBN-13: 978-0-615-31444-0

Library of Congress Catalog Card Number: 2009908033

Book Design by Cecilia Sorochin / SoroDesign

Typeset in Adobe Garamond Pro

Printed in the United States of America

for my family

Journey

Imagine yourself a wandering cloud

With nothing but sky above and below.
Imagine traversing on billows of wind.

Where would you go?

Where would you go?

The Terrible Thing about Cindy

The terrible thing about Cindy
Is she packs a powerful punch.
I learned this yesterday at school
When I tried to take her lunch.

I had only meant to tease her,
To make her squeal and twist.
The last thing I expected
Was her calculated fist.

She socked me in the stomach—
She's more than slightly deft—
And sent me stumbling to my knees,
As she snatched her lunch and left.

After that I was quite sorry
I had tussled with a pro—
I wish my friends had told me
That she practiced tae kwon do.

8

Pull Your Troubles

At night before you sleep, my dears,
You must reach deep inside
And pull your troubles out your ears
Wherein they like to hide.

A trouble is the kind of thing,
It's very often true,
That bothers you more than the soul
Who passed it on to you.

There's something down beneath my bed;
What it is, I'm not quite sure.
But it's only just arrived there;
I'd have noticed it before.
My mother says it's nothing,
And my father shakes his head.
I guess they don't believe in
The thing beneath my bed.

I am sure that it is waiting
Till I turn out the last light
And settle on my pillows
For a very long, dark night.
And when I'm softly drowsing
And my mind is fast asleep,
Out from underneath my bed
That something there will creep.

Something's there

In the morning they'll be sorry
When they find my bunk empty;
They'll know they should have listened—
I was speaking truthfully.
And they'll forever mourn the day
That they simply didn't care
And will always look under their bed,
For a something might be there.

Crabby

I am a crab
Who walks the shore
And pinches toes all day.

If I were you
I'd wear some shoes
And not get in my way.

Your Best

If you always try your best
Then you'll never have to wonder
About what you could have done
If you'd summoned all your thunder.

And if your best
Was not as good
As you hoped it would be,
You still could say,
"I gave today
All that I had in me."

The Eldest

It's just so hard being the eldest;
It's tough always taking the blame;
The younger kids get the attention
And always go first in a game.

I whine just one time and get yelled at;
They do it all day and it's fine;
And toys that once dwelled in *my* room,
I soon find are no longer mine.

My parents' ideas about justice
Are something I simply don't see—
I'm battered for one misdemeanor;
They commit felonies and go free.

And if they, in fact, get in trouble,
I don't have much time to be smug;
Somehow they're still seen as the victims,
While I am observed as a thug.

They make faces and it's "simply charming";
They mess up and it's called a "mistake";
If I blunder there'll be no redemption—
For the eldest, there's never a break.

It's awful the way they must dawdle
And make every errand delayed;
It stinks when you must be their sitter,
As you know that you'll never get paid.

They cry at the drop of a hat,
An obnoxiously loud sort of noise,
Which seems to exclusively stop
When they're offered assortments of toys.

The younger ones' lives are just perfect;
They wake up each day with such glee;
The tough role is being the eldest—
Would you like to trade places with me?

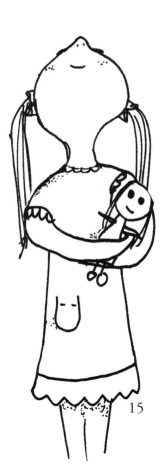

HONEYBEES

Honeybees are a bright sunny yellow,
And they're busy all day with the chore
Of filling their hives up with honey
(I've heard it's a food they adore).

Honeybees all have very sharp stingers;
They don't like invasions of space;
And if you come too near their dwelling,
They'll sting you all over your face.

Magician's Need

A magician with no rabbit's like
A ship without a sail,
A pod without the peas inside,
A shark without a tail.
It's like an oatmeal cookie sans
The raisins and the nuts,
And lacks the thrill of biking on
A road that's full of ruts.

It's a movie without popcorn,
A bash with no balloon;
You wouldn't ask your guests to dine
On soup without a spoon!
A magician needs a rabbit or
His whole act just falls flat—
Nobody cares if you can pull
A walrus from your hat.

The Neighbor's Dog

The neighbor's dog is big and black,
With reddish glowing eyes
That watch you as you're passing,
Awaiting your demise.

The neighbor's dog is rather grim,
With long and piercing claws
That aren't quite so scary
Once you catch sight of his jaws.

His pointy ears are mammoth—
They never miss a sound;
You can be sure he knows it,
If ever you're around.

I'm assuming that they feed him
Only every other day,
'Cause I always see him drooling
When I'm forced to pass this way.

The neighbor's dog is far from cute—
He's not the petting sort;
And if you were to touch him,
You'd come back one hand short.

They sometimes let him out to play—
If he catches you, you're through;
I heard he ate a kid once
(Though I'm not sure if that's true).

If you ever find I'm missing
And you don't know where I've been,
Just ask the neighbor's dog, and
He'll smack his lips and grin.

BEWARE OF DOG!!

Maisy

Maisy always brushed her teeth;
She brushed 'em every day—
Brushed 'em after she ate cake,
And brushed before she'd play,

Scrubbed them right when she got up,
Flossed twice before she slept.
Folks just thought that Maisy liked
To keep her teeth well-kept.

What, perhaps, they didn't know was
Maisy liked the day;
And she'd do all that she could do
To keep the dark at bay.

Maisy cleaned her teeth until
They shone the brightest bright;
So she could smile when nighttime came
And fill her room with light.

Time Out

My watch is quite tired—
It paused at 9:10;
Its ticking just stopped;
It's been snoozing since then.

I've no wish to wake it—
It seems to my mind,
If you're running for hours
You'll need to unwind.

So I'm going to leave it
(I'm not one to harass);
I'll just let it catnap
And be late for class.

The ultimate chocolate chip cookies
Have a center that's gooey and warm;
They are always fresh out of the oven,
With a perfectly circular form.

The ultimate chocolate chip cookies
Have just as much chocolate as dough;
They're cooked to a warm golden brown—
A secret that only moms know.

The Ultimate Chocolate Chip Cookies

The ultimate chocolate chip cookies
Go best with some milk on the side
And always fit well in your pocket
(For the extras you're trying to hide).

And though they say sharing is nice—
And I am inclined to agree—
I must say, I like them the best
When it's only the cookies and me.

Lindsay Nedd

This is the story of Lindsay Nedd,
Whose favorite thing to do was sled.
Every day when it would snow,
She'd grab her coat and off she'd go;
She'd snatch her sled and run kill-dill
To be the first one at the hill,

Then pull her hat over her ears
And tie her scarf real tight,
And brace herself upon her sled,
Preparing for her flight.
Then, leaning forward, off she'd go;
She'd whiz past all the trees
And finally slow down to a stop,
Her face red from the breeze.
She'd grab her sled and climb until
She reached the top once more;
And every time that she'd go down
Was more fun than before.
She'd sled long after other kids
Had gone home wet and cold;
It seemed to her that soaring down
The hill never got old.
And so she'd play until the sun
Had sunk from overhead;
Then she'd race home and brush her teeth
And climb into her bed.

Outside her window snow would fall
Across the street and on her wall;
It kissed the sidewalks and the glass
And piled high upon the grass;
So when she woke, out on the lawn,
There'd be fresh snow to sled upon.

Mr. Caterpillar,

MR. CATERPILLAR

I hope you're happy now—

You've stuffed yourself

All full of leaves;

I'm sure the taste

Was bound to please;

But now I'm on

My hands and knees

Replanting all your chow!

26

Visions

When I lay down upon my bed
And pull the covers o'er my head,
My eyes behold most wondrous things
Such as the daylight never brings.

I don't like peas;
I don't like beans;
I don't like squash
Or other greens.
Instead I'd like
Some cake and pie,
A cone with ice cream
Stacked sky-high.
It seems that when
You're hungriest,
You'd eat the foods
You like the best.
So pass the sprinkles,
If you please,
And pass the pie,
But keep your peas.

DOWN WITH GREENS

Sick

Don't breathe next to me!
You might get me sick.
Your nose is so red
That it looks like a brick.

Your eyes are all puffy;
You're sneezing a lot.
I'm leaving the room;
I don't want what you've got.

Don't cough when I'm here—
You might pass it on.
For goodness sakes,
Cover your mouth when you yawn!

And don't touch my food,
Lest your cooties adhere,
Thus making me sick
For the rest of the year.

The last thing I need
Is a cold or a flu,
And so I am thinking
I'll bid you adieu.

I'm much better off
Wherever you're not—
Don't breathe next to me;
I don't want what you've got!

Bird Song

Twee! Twee! Twee!

Little bird,

I only wish I knew

The meaning of your warblings

So I could **twee** with you.

IQ Test

I don't think I did so well;
I didn't know too much . . .
I did what I could;
I tried as I should;
But a test hard as that
Can come to no good.
So when my score comes
And you're not too impressed,
Please keep in mind
That I did my best.

Sandwich Sister

My sister is made of her favorite foods:
Peanut butter and jelly;
This all came about from indulging
Her sandwich-craving belly.

She didn't used to be this way—
She used to look alright—
Till she ate one bite too many,
Then up and changed one night.

She did not go unwarned,
As Mom would often say,
"If you keep on eating that,
You'll turn into it one day."

But still she didn't listen,
And every lunch she spread
Her peanut butter and jelly
Between two hunks of bread,

Then cut it into triangles,
And set them on her plate,
And poured herself a glass of milk,
And every bite she ate.

Then one evening she looked sick.
"I don't feel so good," she said;
And, not desiring dinner,
She went upstairs to bed.

In the morning when I saw her
As she tottered down the stair,
Instead of being somewhat round,
She was looking rather square.

Needless to say, I was worried
When she sat at the table and cried
About how her skin was now bread
With peanuts and jelly inside.

Still, she's adapted nicely,
And I am proud to say
That she doesn't let the transformation
Get into her way.

She is the smartest sandwich
In our entire school,
And her delectable appearance
Makes all the fellows drool.

But she must avoid the rain
(Being soggy's what she hates most)
And not spend much time in the sun
(In the heat she tends to toast).

The moral of the story,
As everyone might guess,
Is *never eat your favorite food*
In everyday excess.

GOOD THINGS

I once heard an old man say,
Shaping vases out of clay
Into subtle forms sublime,

" Listen, son, good things take time. "

All my life I've thought of this
When a task was lacking bliss,
When the work seemed awfully tough
And I thought I'd had enough.

So I'd give a little more
To what sometimes seemed a chore;
And, you know, without a doubt,
Good things always came about.

I Ate a **Chili Pepper**

I ate a chili pepper
On a lunch-time dare;
Sandy said I'd burn my mouth,
But I didn't care.

I ate that chili pepper—
Left not a seed to waste—
And won that truly silly bet,
But lost my sense of taste.

39

Snow Day

In the winter it's every kid's dream,
As snowflakes begin to appear,
That suddenly there'll be a blizzard,
And they'll cancel school for the year.

Though most kids are willing to settle,
And I am inclined to agree,
They could merely close school for one day—
One day off would be just fine with me.

A day free from all forms of homework,
A day without science or math,
When you leave all your school books at home—
And run out the door with a laugh.

A day full of sledding and cocoa
And snowmen who wear Dad's old clothes;
No writing out boring equations
After lunch when you'd rather just doze.

A snow day's a day meant for lounging,
Where idleness isn't condemned,
A day where you sleep in till lunchtime,
A day that you don't want to end.

And if you are truly quite lucky,
The snow will continue its flight,
And you'll spend the afternoon hoping
The next day will be just as white.

Surprise

They rolled their eyes and groaned
And quickly grabbed their books,
Flipping through the pages
For a few last, fleeting looks.

They grumbled and they cringed,
And all gave evil eyes;
They whispered to their neighbors;
They filled the room with sighs.

"I knew that this would happen"
Could be heard throughout the room;
And they sharpened up their pencils,
As they all foresaw their doom.

They squawked and moaned and sniveled—
They made every sound there is—
The day their teacher told them
They'd be having a pop quiz.

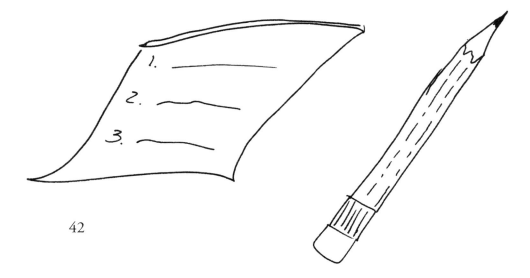

A Thought

There's dirt beneath my nails
That comes from my travails.
And though at supper I must clean
The evidence of where I've been,
I must say that it seems obscene
To dwell on such details.

My Brother's Bike

My brother has the neatest bike that I have ever seen—
It's got ten gears and two red lights, and it's metallic green.
My brother rides that bike of his every day to school;
Needless to say, because of it, he's superlatively cool.
He never lets me touch it (my greatest of desires),
But sometimes he will let me help pump air into the tires.

I'd like to think my brother is an understanding guy—
The sort who tends to keep his calm when something goes awry.
I'm hoping that he'll see his bike and try to understand
That life without something that cool can be a little bland.
Then maybe he'll contain himself and his ferocity
When he finds I took it for a ride and crashed into a tree.

TALL

I'm thinking sequoia;
I'm thinking the moon;
I'm thinking tall thoughts
So I'll grow pretty soon.

I'm thinking giraffe
Or a giant plateau;
And the taller I think,
The higher I'll grow.

Mansions and flagpoles
Are tall in their rights;
It's all in perspective
When dealing with heights.

I can feel myself stretch
As I sit here and speak;
Pretty soon folks will notice
My lofty physique.

I am thinking tall thoughts;
Being small's such a bore;
By tomorrow giraffes
Won't seem tall anymore.

A Good Day

Today will be a good day,
And I will make it so—
I cannot make the sun come out;
I cannot make the flowers sprout;
I cannot make the fishes bite,
Nor blow the wind beneath my kite.
But I can wear a friendly smile
And listen to the trees a while
And laugh real loud and run real fast
And make each moment such a blast.
I can sing though skies be gray,
'Cause I am captain of my day.

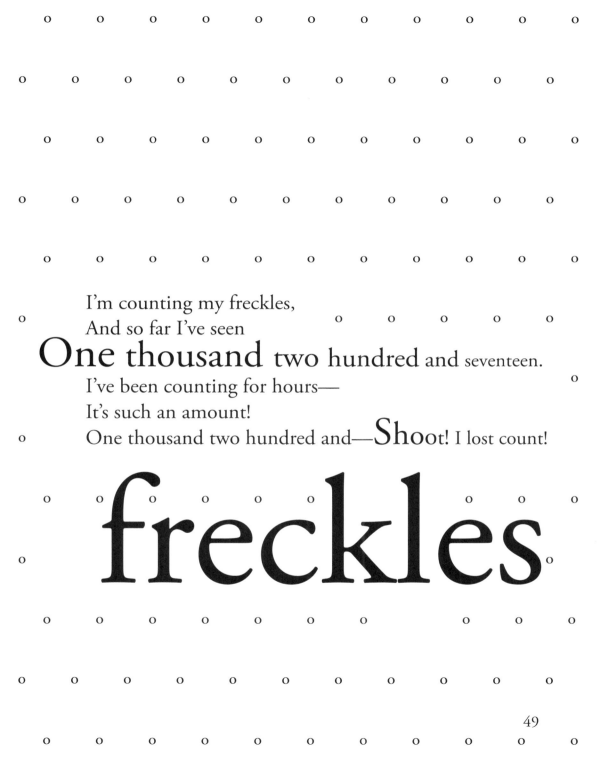

I'm counting my freckles,
And so far I've seen
One thousand two hundred and seventeen.
I've been counting for hours—
It's such an amount!
One thousand two hundred and—Shoot! I lost count!

freckles

49

The Masters of Balledere Hall

We're the masters of Balledere Hall.
We live feast-to-feast, brawl-to-brawl.
We fight by the sword,
Nay, for love nor reward,
But for the sheer thrill of it all.

We're comrades-in-arms, every one.
We won't quit a duel once begun.
As we parry, we grin
And our skills revel in;
For us, fighting foes is sheer fun.

We won't leave a lady distraught,
Won't rest till her captors are caught.
But once we relieve her,
We rapidly leave her,
For most women come with a knot.

Such typified gents all are we—
Refined and well-bred to a T.
We bow with such grace,
Every eye in the place
Can see our supreme pedigree.

We're practically royal, you know.
Kings greet us wherever we go.
We're known through the land
For our generous hand,
So grand are the gifts we bestow.

We're the masters of Balledere Hall.
For all that is right, we stand tall.
Defending the meek
Is a typical week;
If ever you need us, just call.

New Shoes

I got new shoes—
The kind the kids
All want to wear at school,

The ones the sports star
Says are great—
These shoes are flat-out cool.

I told my mom
I needed them;
I had to have this pair.

The only problem
With them is
They're such a pain to wear!

Willow

The branches on a willow tree
Hang over low for you and me
To grab a-hold and swing and swing
Until the dinner bell doth ring.

Sweet Dreams

If the ocean were of chocolate milk
And the sand were sugar grains,
If the sky were frosted-icing blue
And sprinkled gumdrop rains,

Then my ship would be a ginger snap,
Which rolled on whipped cream waves;
And cotton candy sails would lead
To peanut brittle caves.

55

Braces

I went to the doctor today;
He said braces would make me look charming.
But, frankly, once they had been glued there,
My appearance became quite alarming.

This metal all over my mouth
Hurts almost as bad as it looks.
I think that the doctor's insane,
Despite his degrees and his books.

The next time I go in to see him
And he flashes that big, phony grin,
I know that inside I'll be wishing
The braces instead were on him.

M*is*m*a*tched

I have a box
That's full of socks,
And no two are the same;
And so I'll wear
A mismatched pair—
It's really quite a shame.

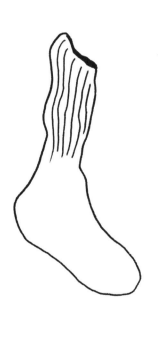

PANTRY PARTY

In the dark of the night
After you've gone to sleep,
Out of the cupboard
The cookies will creep.

They'll sound the alarm
To come one and all—
The time has arrived
For their midnight ball!

Then all through the kitchen
The foods come alive—
The apples and peanuts
And cupcakes (all five).

Potatoes roll over
And open their eyes;
They call to their tots
And the wavy French fries.

The chilies all salsa;
The corn lends an ear
To the veal who is singing
Of the one he holds dear.

The rolls are all rising
To see what they can
Of all the commotion
From their warm little pan.

Ricotta and cheddar
All smile and say *CHEESE!*
While the milk takes their picture
With their good friends, the peas.

The hominy hang out
With tortilla folks,
Who all are amazed
By their strange, corny jokes.

Then the veggies compete
In a race for the cup
And as beans take the lead,
The tomatoes catch up.

But, all of a sudden,
They notice the sun,
And each must return
To where he came from.

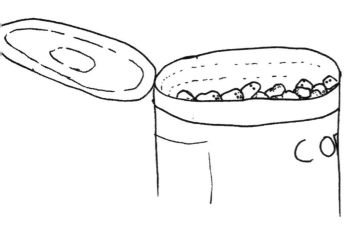

They tiptoe to freezers
And silently climb
Back into their places
At just the right time.

Then all through the day
They patiently wait
For their party to start
When it's once again late.

A Plan

I'm painting my room on some cardboard.
(My plan's really ingenious, you know.)
So the next time my mom wants my room clean,
I'll just prop up my mural and go.

What happened to all my belongings?
With art this detailed she won't guess
That my aesthetic genius deceived her,
With a drawing that hides the big mess.

a Penguin's Perspective

Said one penguin to another,
" This cold weather's not for me.
If it weren't for my egg here,
I'd be off in Waikiki. "

DENNIS EDMONDS
FETTLESBERRY

I'm Dennis Edmonds Fettlesberry,
And I've memorized the dictionary.

Though a protracted task, I must say,
It has been most salubrious
In affecting how I confabulate
In discourse far less dubious.

My contemporaries' opinions
And mine do not conform;
Their lackadaisical orations
Are distressingly the norm.

The hackneyed slang which turns up
In most conversations today
Is scarcely the way to deliver
Asseverations one has to say.

And though my refined ways of speaking
Intermittently draw aberrant looks,
I find I exude the intelligence
Of one who's construed many books.

All these scholastic expressions
Are magnificent, delightful to use;
Now if you will please excuse me—
I've a thesaurus to peruse.

Cocoa Stand

My cocoa stand's not too successful,
Though I cannot understand why.
It seems that nobody wants cocoa
On a hot afternoon in July.

Steaming Hot
Chocolate--
~~50¢~~ ~~25¢~~ 10¢

A WARNING

Take heed on every windy day

To tie a rock upon your shoe,

So that you do not blow away

And whiffle off into the blue.

Suzie Bitner was afraid of the Drain

Suzie Bitner was afraid of the drain, and so she never showered,
And consequently smelled like milk that was left too long—and soured.
"I simply won't go near the tub," she pinched her face and cried.
"The moment I turn the water on, it will suck me down inside!"

Her mother pleaded with her, but from bathing she abstained;
Her father, he implored her, but her stubbornness remained.
And so it came to pass that she grew dirtier by the day.
And all her friends stopped calling or coming by to play.

Suzie grew quite lonely in her slimy, smelly state
And finally thought her choice, she'd re-evaluate.
"Okay, okay, I'll take a bath!" she sniffed through muddy tears;
And, bar of soap in shaking hand, she went to face her fears.

But the water felt so nice to her when steaming, piping hot
That all her dismal drainage dread, Suzie then forgot;
And never ever more was scared to climb into the tub
And give her little body a flawless, thorough scrub.

Now she washes till her skin has a pinkish sort of glow.
And everybody says that she's the cleanest girl they know.

A Memory

Remember the time that we sat and we ate
Two lemon cupcakes from a silvery plate?
Remember we toasted to you and to me,
The things we had done and the places we'd see?
How we each raised our treats and tapped them like wine—
My icing on yours, your icing on mine?
Remember that bright sugar-filled afternoon?
No, neither do I; but come . . . we will soon.

shhh!
When in the library.

shhh!
When Grandma's having tea.

shhh!
When baby's fast asleep;
Not a noise—not a peep.

shhh!
shhh!
When Dad gets home from work.

shhh!
Or he will go berserk.

shhh!
When it is time for bed.

shhh! shhh! shhh!
My mother said.

But you know what's such a riot?
All her shushing's sure not quiet.

DEAR SANTA

Dear Santa,

I know that the holiday season
Is your busiest time of the year,
So I've made up a list to assist you,
With the hope that it's perfectly clear:

One princess ballerina doll (the one with curly hair),
A pair of skates, a pogo stick, one fuzzy teddy bear,
A pink snow cap with matching gloves, a puppy in a box,
A stocking with my favorite sweets, a brand new set of blocks;
I want another china doll (I dropped the one I had;
I tried to make her better, but the injury was bad).
A set of drums, a big doll house, a new bell for my bike,
The sweater that my best friend has (so we can look alike),
A great big pack of bubble gum (I chew it every day),
A radio, a telescope, a massive wad of clay.

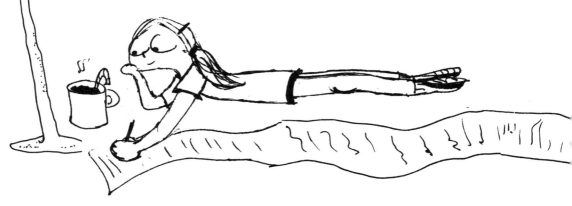

I'd like to have a wallet (with money would be nice),
And also a machine that makes big snow cones out of ice.
Some pink fur boots, and paper dolls, and board games stacked sky-high,
A jump rope and a hula-hoop, a kite that I can fly,
The fastest sled in all the world, a bouncy ball or two,
A big notepad, and glitter pens, some scissors, tape, and glue;
I want a chocolate-colored horse that I can ride to school;
I also think that I'd enjoy a brand new swimming pool.
Puzzles, ribbons for my hair, a journal with a lock,
Picture books, a painting set, my very own pet rock,
A snow globe that plays music when you wind it up real tight,
A soft stuffed moose that I can hold when I get scared at night;
A new swing set and curly slide would just be so much fun;
A checkers board, and dresses, and stickers by the ton.
I think I've covered everything; that's all that I can list—
Feel free to just surprise me if you think of things I've missed.

Mice
on
ROLLER SKATES

Mice on roller skates
Deflect our traps with ease.
They're fast;
    They're furry
        And furious,
And always get their cheese.

Grandpa

I asked my grandpa
What it's like
To feel real old and slow.

He shook his head
And smiled and said,
" I'll tell you when I know. "

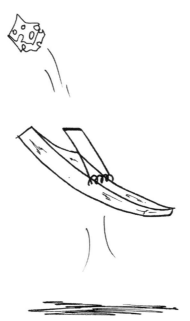

The Very Best Climber

I'm the very best climber you ever did see;
I climbed by myself to the top of this tree.
I mounted the base and ascended some more,
Then paused halfway up 'cause my arms just got sore.
And, once I was rested, I scaled higher still
And was feeling quite proud, as this sport takes some skill.
I shimmied myself all the way to the top;
There was no more to climb, so I chose then to stop.

But now, as I look out from such a great height,
I find that my stomach does not feel quite right.
The excitement I'd felt, I must meekly confess,
Has now been replaced with a shocking distress.
I'm thinking a ladder might just do the trick;
If somebody has one, please bring it here quick!
I'm the very best climber in all of our town,
But the one skill I'm lacking is how to get down.

My Sister Plays Piano

My sister plays piano;
She's played it for three years.
I hope she plans on quitting,
And so do both my ears.

Jack-O-Lantern

The sprightly Jack-O-Lantern's eyes
Glow with knowledge, I surmise,
Of the tricks that make men fools,
From the local ghosts and ghouls.

There is a house

There is a house,
A yellow house,
Atop a winding lane
Where dwells a man
Who drives to work
And then drives back again.
And in this house,
This yellow house,
Live thirty-six pet mice
Who help to clean
The travertine
And keep it looking nice.
And in the yard,
A great big yard,
Are thirteen hungry sheep
Who feed upon
The grassy lawn
And rarely make a peep.
A spider on
The weathervane
Keeps close watch on the sky
And always knows
If there'll be snows
Or if it will be dry.
It's curious
The way they live—
A happy, motley clan—
With each one there
Doing his share
The very best he can.

STOP TALKING!

You talk too much! You talk too much!
Can you have this much to say?
You start the minute you get up
And blab throughout the day.

I've never met another soul
Who yaps as much as you;
And every time I think you're done
I find you're still not through.

You talk too much! Silence
Is something you don't know;
And so you chatter on and on
'Most everywhere you go.

With all the things you have to say
It seems like you would pop;
You talk too much—I beg you—
Please close your mouth and stop.

I cannot take it anymore;
My ears hurt to the touch;
I think I've made it very clear—
You absolutely talk too much!

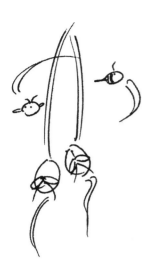

Two Tennies

Two white tennies
Off for a walk,
Skip for a mile,
Run for a block.
Race 'round the park,
Wind through the trees,
Splash in the creek,
Dance with the bees.
Zip 'round the playground,
Jump over logs,
Drum down the sidewalk
Chased by two dogs.
Two muddy tennies,
Tired from their play,
Wipe 'cross the mat
And call it a day.

VALENTINE

Today I wrote a valentine
For pretty Mandy Slater
And slipped it in her locker
With the hope she'd find it later.

I poured my very soul out
Into each and every line;
With such a composition,
There's no way she won't be mine.

I carefully selected
All the perfect words to say—
How her presence in the classroom
Always brightens up my day.

With her brilliant bluish eyes
And her silky golden hair,
There's no way the other girls
Could aspire to compare.

I conveyed to her how fortune
Had smiled on me in math,
As the seating chart had placed her
Very nearly in my path:

Sitting two seats to the left
And nearly three rows forward,
I can stare at her through class
Without ever being bored.

And how her lilting laughter
Makes a beat skip in my heart,
And the loneliness I feel
Every time we are apart.

Every sentence was sheer genius;
All my words were so exact—
I can't wait for her to read it
And to see how she'll react.

I sealed it in an envelope
And propelled it through her door;
And, though it's not addressed to her,
She'll know just who it's for.

Still, now that I am sitting here,
The more and more I wait,
It seems as though I can't recall
If it's locker four or eight.

It's locker eight, I'm pretty sure;
I guess I'll wait and see,
Though I'm curious to know
Why Dan's glowering at me.

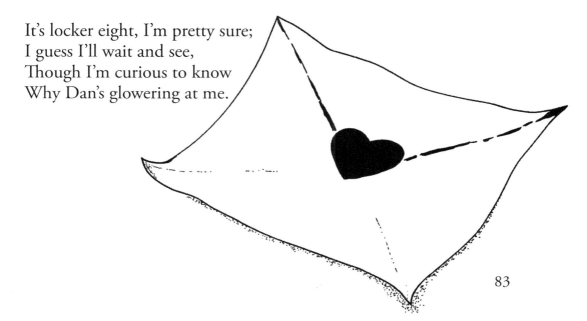

My Brother
Is Driving Me
Crazy

My brother is driving me crazy;
He does everything that I do.
Whenever I wear my team jacket,
My brother must wear his coat, too.

Whenever I want to go biking,
My brother is always in tow.
And when I feel up for some ice cream,
My brother nods, face all aglow.

I can't travel off on my own now
'Cause he always has to join in;
And now he is sporting my haircut,
Much to my total chagrin.

I wish he would try a bit harder
To be just himself and not me;
But each time I want for some distance,
I find it is hard to break free.

Perhaps we should move to the Arctic,
Where reindeer and polar bears rule.
I'm sure, in a land that is frigid,
I won't be the only one cool.

Thundercloud

Nobody likes a thundercloud,
But everyone loves the sun;
I wish I'd been a ray of light,
'Cause thunderclouds aren't much fun.

Two
Gibbons Reach
for the Moon

There once were two gibbons
High up in a tree
Who stared out before them,
And what did they see?

Not the fields, nor the haystacks,
The June bugs in June;
No, the gibbons instead
Fixed their eyes on the moon.

"How delicious!" they cried,
"Such a round, perfect sphere.
Let's reach out and snatch it,
For it looks very near."

So one gibbon swung down,
For the moon hung quite low,
And he stretched, and he strained
Far as his arm would go.

But, try as he might,
It avoided his grasp;
And he wiped at his brow
And then said with a gasp,

"It's just slightly too far,
Just a hair, just a bit;
I am sure if you help me
We two could reach it."

So, forming a chain,
One ape hung from the other
And lunged once again
As he clung to his brother.

"It is just a smidge far,
Just a sliver, a tad.
Let us find one more friend,
And it won't be so bad."

So the two became three,
Became four, became ten;
But the moon seemed to skirt off
Again and again.

Still, the gibbons keep trying.
They strain in the dark,
And each time they find
They are shy of the mark.

They gather in daylight
And rest when it's noon;
But once nighttime comes,
They all reach for the moon.

RAKING LEAVES

I raked the leaves on our front lawn;
It took all afternoon.
I started at 'round half past one
and said, "I'll be done soon."

But once I saw how more leaves fell
Each time I made a pile,
I quickly saw this outdoor chore
Was going to take a while.

And so I did what my dad said
A winner does to win:
I studied that great pile of leaves,
And then I jumped right in.

Strange Girl

What do you do if the girl next to you has an extra eye on her face?
Do you sit there and stare, or play unaware, or focus on some other place?
What do you say if the girl next to you has skin that's a bright, flashy green?
Can you ask if she's sick and not feeling too well, or will she think you're being mean?
What do you say if she sizes you up and says you're a fine specimen?
And if an antenna protrudes from her head and wiggles out signals, what then?
How do you act if she leaves all her food and instead eats her fork and her spoon?
What do you say to her curious face when she asks why you're leaving so soon?

White Noise

In all the world
There's nothing like
The sound of falling snow—

The only noise
I've ever known
That makes the clocks move slow;

The only sound
That sweeps away
The din of city streets;

And wraps around,
In soft embrace,
'Most everyone it meets;

A sound that's not
A sound at all—
A quiet, soft and dear,

That comforts all
The sleepy souls
Who sit, and watch, and hear.

Ode
to Sugar Flakes

Sugar flakes, I adore you—you're crunchy and sweet—
You make every morning I wake up complete.
The sweeter your flakes are, the less I resist;
And, once I start eating, I cannot desist.

There's nothing quite like you—you're one of a kind—
You're sugar, contentment, and comfort combined.
You're good when you're dry, and you crunch with each bite;
And when you're with milk, you are such a delight!

Some people like muffins or cherry crumb cake
Or pancakes stacked high in a syrupy lake,
But foods such as these make my stomach distressed—
Leave me sullen and hungry and highly depressed.

You won't find me making those breakfast mistakes;
I intend to stay faithful to my sugar flakes.
Sugar flakes, you're the greatest; you make my life whole;
You look swell in your box and superb in my bowl.

You give my life meaning and make each day new;
Sugar flakes, you're stupendous—I truly love you.

Tire
Swing

Twisting,
Turning,
Spinning,
Sliding.

Swinging,
Laughing,
Rocking,
Gliding.

Lurching,
Reeling,
Undulating.

Jumping
Offing,
Contemplating.

Nauseous
Stomach
Detonating!

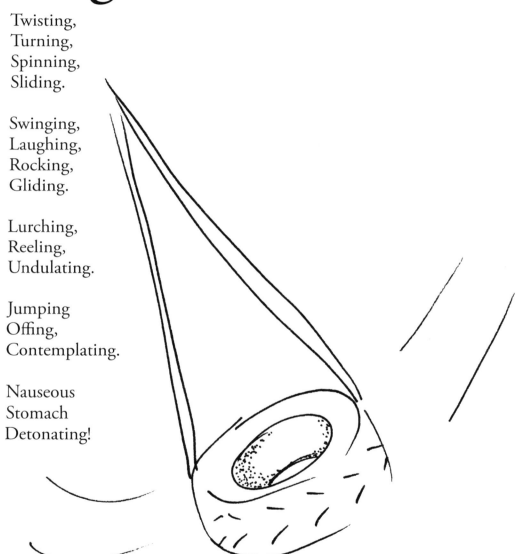

Mr. Happenstance

If you should go
Where the wild winds blow,
Where the cattails play
And the skybirds dance,

Would you stop
And say hello
To my friend,
Mr. Happenstance?

The Great Ant Attack

It was the perfect Saturday—
The sky was blue, the sun was bright—
The kind that begs *come out and play*,
So we grabbed our lunches and our kite.

We headed for the nearest park
And found the perfect place to sit
And opened all the plasticware
For the perfect lunch we planned to split.

When out from underneath a bush
One small, black ant began to crawl;
We gave it no more than a glance—
Who's scared of things that are that small?

But, not long after it appeared,
Another ant poked out its head;
And soon there was a line of them
All heading toward our stack of bread.

We tried to blow their squad away,
But that did not work out too well;
We dug a mini bug-like trench
And one-by-one watched as they fell.

"Ha-ha!" we laughed—success was ours;
Those ants would not shoplift our lunch;
How rude of them to sneak about—
They are a surreptitious bunch.

We started munching cookies first
(You must start picnics with a snack);
We ate in bliss, quite unaware,
The ants were planning their attack.

About ten bites into our meal
We noticed something rather weird—
It seemed as though our bag of chips
And onion dip had disappeared.

We looked about but could not find
The missing chips and dip we brought;
And, as these are our favorite foods,
The four of us were quite distraught.

A rustling sound behind my back
Gave cause for me to turn around.
And there it was! Our bag of chips—
Moving swiftly on the ground!

Carted off by small black ants—
The thieves! How dare they steal our stuff?
Then they returned to take some more;
Our chips and dip were not enough.

And what had been one trail of bugs
Augmented to a troop or two;
We huddled in a tiny bunch
And pondered just what we should do.

Just seconds later we were trapped
And much more frightened than before;
What started as a minor tiff
Had grown into a full-scale war!

The ants poured out from all around;
They took our cupcakes and our jam.
They carried off our cheese and fruit
And even stole our slice of ham.

And when the last crumb from our cake
Was purloined from our picnic site,
The ants retreated with their spoils
To celebrate throughout the night.

The next time that you make a lunch
And take it to the park to snack,
Remember that the ants live there
And watch out 'cause they might attack!

Snow Kisses

If you go out when it's snowing
And look up at the sky,
You'll feel lots of icy kisses
As the snowflakes flutter by.

Bored

This book is very long,
And I'm just on page two—
With many more to go
And better things to do.

I could be outside playing
And sunning in the sun
And eating melted ice cream
And other stuff that's fun.

Instead I'm reading something
As exciting as a flea—
Wishing I were somewhere else . . .
At least I'm on page three.

Fishing

My dad wanted us to go fishing;
"It's a father and son thing," he said;
But we have been here for three hours,
And I think that the fish must be dead.

We have not had one single nibble—
Not a bite or a chomp or a munch;
Maybe they had a big breakfast
And just aren't hungry for lunch.

My dad doesn't seem the least anxious;
He says, "Patience will be our reward";
But sitting here watching the water
Has left me remarkably bored.

The sun's sliding out of the sky now,
And I think that it's time we went back;
We can stop by the store on the way there
And purchase the fish that we lack.

We load up the car to head home in;
"That was fun," my dad says with a smile;
And suddenly my afternoon
Went from humdrum to pretty worthwhile.

It's
Raining
Hearts

It's raining hearts;
It's storming flowers;
We're in for scattered
Stardust showers.

It's drizzling chocolate,
Pouring pies;
We might be seeing
Candy skies.

Of all the weather
There could be,
Plain water seems
A waste to me.

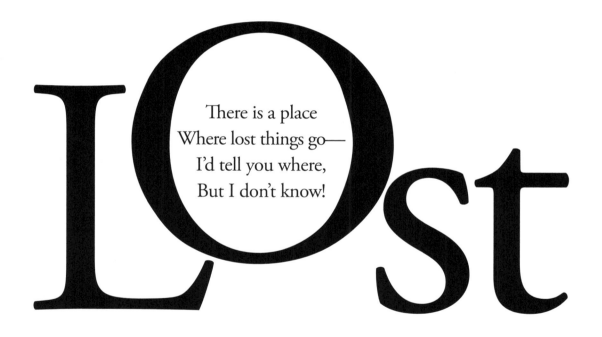

L**O**st

There is a place
Where lost things go—
I'd tell you where,
But I don't know!

The Baseball Flew Out of the Park

The baseball flew out of the park.
It blasted clean over the fence.
It shot through the leaves
On Ms. McCrae's trees,
And no one has seen the thing hence.

The baseball lit out with a crack.
It vanished in two seconds flat.
And those there that day
Will whisper and say
They saw smoke rise up from the bat.

It went down in Little League fame.
They say the ball's traveling still.
At the rate which it flew,
It is now in Peru
And will soon be traversing Brazil.

I'm charting the course it will take,
Providing its route stays the same.
It should be back here
At this time next year,
And then we can finish our game.

Fast
Friends

Said the turtle to the sloth,
"You are awfully, awfully slow."
And the sloth, he thought a moment,
And he smiled and said, "I know."

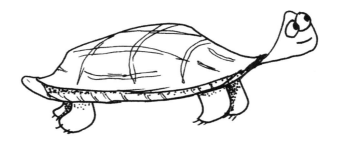

Then the sloth said to the turtle,
"You are not so very fast."
And the two of them decided
Here's a friendship that would last.

SHARING

This half of the room is mine,
And your half's over there;
I've marked the border clearly
Just to make sure things stay fair.

This line divides the sloppy
From the tidy and the clean;
It separates the scummy
From all that is pristine.

No longer will I find your shoes
Amassed under *my* bed;
Your sandals, boots, and sneakers
Will remain with you instead.

Your clothes and books and cookie crumbs
Will all stay on *your* side;
And don't think I won't confiscate
What crosses the divide.

And though the door's on my side,
I've been most neighborly
In leaving you full access
Of the window by the tree.

I trust you'll manage nicely—
Climbing in and out—
With all this sunny weather
It is quite the scenic route.

I've compiled a list of rules
To which you must adhere;
I think you'll understand them all,
As I've made them very clear.

I think I've covered everything;
That's all I have to say.
So, if you have no questions,
Would you like to come and play?

Boomerang

Nobody told me a boomerang
Would turn and come back to you.
I'm sorry now I used such force
When I aimed at Ted and threw.

Patience

Patience is waiting for dinner to end
So you can start eating ice cream;
Patience is yearning for daylight to leave
So you can get back to your dream.

Patience is coping with your little sis
Who's slowing the rest of you down;
Patience is hoping the cookies you bake
Will hurry along and get brown.

And while this control can so often
Be tiring and trying, it's true,
We find it's expected from others
For all of the things that *we* do.

It seems that the only solution
(I certainly hope you agree)
Is *I'll show some patience with you,*
If you'll show some patience with me.

MR. PICKINILLY

Mr. Pickinilly
Loves to eat his cheese.
Quite a connoisseur is he
Of provolones and Bries.
He loves his mozzarella,
And Gouda from the Dutch,
But will not lay a hand on Swiss
'Cause he won't get as much.

My Dad Made my Lunch

My dad made my lunch—
He meant to be sweet,
But the meal that he packed
I'm not sure I can eat.

He spread peanut butter
On two chunks of bread
In such ample amounts
If I eat it I'm dead.

For I fear that my jaws,
At the very first bite,
Would be so overwhelmed
That they'd seal up real tight.

In place of the chips,
Which I usually get,
Is an apple that looks
Like it's not ripe just yet.

And, rather than milk,
My thermos contains
A vegetable juice
With carrot remains.

The only thing tasty
I have here to eat
Is some chocolate cake,
Which I know is a treat.

But, sadly, it's smashed
By the thermos of juice;
I've never known cake
To see such abuse.

I know my dad thought
This was food I preferred;
And he tried really hard,
So I won't say a word.

But I have been thinking,
And I have a hunch,
That starting tomorrow
I'll make my own lunch.

Sun is hot;

Rain is wet;

Clouds are just plain dreary.

Sleet feels nasty;

Hail is hard;

sun is hot

Snow is cold and bleary.

Thunder's loud;

Wind's a mess;

Storms prohibit play.

I guess I'll stay inside until

This weather goes away.

Night Dreams

I'd like to think that I could fly,
To lift my feet and touch the sky,
To soar above, look down below,
And never know just where I'd go.

And if I could, oh what I'd see!
Earth would not be the same to me.

Oh, if the wind would carry two,
I'd hope that I could fly with you;
And hand-in-hand we'd chase the stars
And lock them up in pickle jars.

We'd laugh and smile, then set them free
To twinkle for eternity.

Worms for Pets

I don't have a dog;
I don't have a cat;
I don't have a fish
Or a bird or a rat.

Instead of these pets,
I have worms in a jar;
They can't catch a ball,
And they don't run real far.

They don't jump to see me
(In fact, I'm ignored);
It's not real exciting
Unless I am bored.

I'd wanted a puppy,
A gerbil, or mouse—
A pet that would follow me
All through the house.

But Mom didn't seem
To be keen on this thought;
She said I could have worms,
So it's worms that I got.

My worms don't make noise;
They do no real work;
They don't get offended
When friends point and smirk.

It's not too much fun;
It's as dull as it gets
To be the kid who
Has worms for her pets.

Catch of the Day

The fisherman, casting his net very wide,
Will find lots of fishes are tangled inside.
The fisherman, casting his net very small,
Will wind up with pebbles or nothing at all.

The Christmas Lights Went Out

The Christmas lights went out—
The ones Dad just suspended.
He took all day to hang them,
But their gleaming's promptly ended.

I wonder how he'll take it
When he steps out in the snow
To marvel at his handiwork
But find he's missed the show.

The Christmas lights went out,
And all's dark on our lawn—
One fleeting, fizzling moment
And his masterpiece is gone.

I think I'll step inside now
To avoid how he reacts
When he finds one broken bulb
In the middle of my tracks.

123

A Ghost Who Loves the Movies

I'm a ghost who loves the movies;
I never miss a show.
I pour myself some popcorn
And sit in the front row.

I just adore the comedies
And laugh the whole way through;
The last time I saw one of those,
I laughed away my **BOO.**

I like to watch the dramas,
And musicals are fun,
But fall asleep in mushy flicks
The moment they've begun.

But mostly I prefer the films
That chill you to the bone—
The kind that leave you wishing
That you had not come alone.

It seems folks don't appreciate
A movie-going shade;
They say I scare the crowds away
And make people afraid.

Though I'm as friendly as can be
And always say **_hello_**
To those who sit right next to me
Before they start the show.

I'm a ghost who loves the movies;
It's my favorite place to be;
So the next time that you see one,
You might bump into me.

Daydream

Windows were meant for wandering eyes
On languorous days with sunshiny skies,
For dreams of adventure in lands far away,
For fleeting cloud-pictures that never do stay.

A pause from the current, a break from the flow,
A place where the lessons and homework can't go;
So don't take offense if you see my gaze stray—
That's just the effect of a day like today.

Upside-Down

I woke up upside-down;
I don't know how I did.
All I can say
Is that today
I've really flipped my lid.

I woke up wrong-side-down.
It's really quite bizarre.
And from this view,
I'm telling you,
You can't see very far.

I woke up in a twist;
I flat-out woke up wrong.
I'm going back
To bed until
I'm back where I belong!

❧ *Girls* ❧

I simply don't understand girls;
I don't understand them at all—
The way they are never alone
And travel in packs down the hall.

Or why they all whisper and giggle
And pass secret notes on the side
And always use colorful pens
To write stuff they're trying to hide.

Their papers are constantly covered
With masses of tiny pink hearts;
You'd think they'd be more interested
In racecars and aeroplane parts.

They don't care a thing about baseball;
They never play "soldiers" or "war";
They snub any form of explosion
And view watching football a chore.

But mostly I don't understand
How, despite all the things that they lack,
I'd love to say *hi* to the girls
And watch as they'd all say *hi* back.

I don't think I've had this much trouble
With anything I can recall;
Girls really are difficult people;
I don't understand girls at all.

Stinky Feet

My mom says I have stinky feet,
But I don't think that's true.
Could you bend down and smell them, please,
And tell me if I do?

Don't Rush Me, Please

I am a snail—
Don't rush me, please.
I'm heading for
Those cherry trees.

I have no place
I have to be,
No pressing thing
I have to see.

I like this speed;
I like being slow;
It gives me time
To get to know

All the flowers
That I pass,
Every blade
Of every grass.

I am a snail;
This is my way.
Don't rush me, please.
We've got all day.

Dinah

Dinah *loved* nothing more than to dress up,
And so she spent most of her days
Making costumes of clothes in the attic
And putting on whimsical plays.

She'd wrap herself up in a towel
And slip on an old pair of shorts
And traipse from the den to the kitchen
Claiming she was a princess, of sorts.

She'd wear rubber boots and a raincoat
And play weatherman in a storm,
Or pull on her fluffy pink tutu
And ask that folks watch her perform.

She'd garnish her hair with some jewelry
And allege fairy status to all,
Then slide 'round in soft, fuzzy slippers
And exclaim she could fly down the hall.

It made Dinah smile quite often
To think of the things she could be
And dream of the places she'd go
And wonder what people she'd see.

Her parents thought it quite amusing
To hear her excitedly state
Occupations she found fascinating
And attempted to then re-create.

It seemed to them such an amazement
That old clothes could bring so much bliss;
They laughed at all her make-believings
And said, "She'll soon tire of this."

But long after most other children
Had laid their pretending to rest,
Little Dinah continued her dreaming
And decided it's what she liked best.

So she found in the world all around her
A magic that most can't conceive;
It's a pleasure we all can partake in
If we let ourselves simply believe.

NOISY BUGS

Why do cicadas
Banter at night?
You sleep when it's dark;
You chat when it's light.

But no one informed
Cicadas of this,
And so every evening
They click and they hiss.

If some of the more polite
Insects out there
Would tell them to hush up
And be more aware,

Perhaps they would clam up
And not speak a peep;
And then we could all
Get a little more sleep.

Wood Siren

There is a spider in our wood
Who spins a web of gold;
She draws insects from miles around
That keep her fed, I'm told.

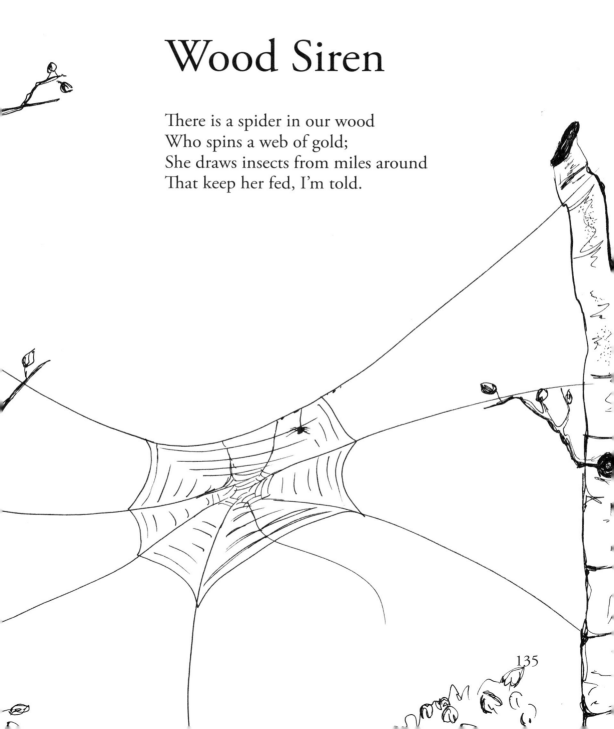

135

Molehills

Don't make a mountain out of a molehill
is very trite advice
when you've every reason to be mad
and, therefore, not so nice.

But I've been told, and I believe—
The story's good as true—
That molehills can, in fact, increase
When folks make much ado.

It happened very long ago
In a town called Ungralee
That no one seemed to get along,
And no one could agree.

And so they fought 'most all the time,
And each would have a fit.
And every time one said, "No fair!"

A molehill grew a bit.

Until the molehills swelled so large
There was no place to live;
And so the townsfolk moved away,
Unable to forgive.

They scattered in all directions
And took with them dissent
Which they will share with anyone
Who'll listen to them vent.

Next time you hear someone complain
And whine and stamp and crow,
Take one step back—no, make it two—
And watch the molehill grow.

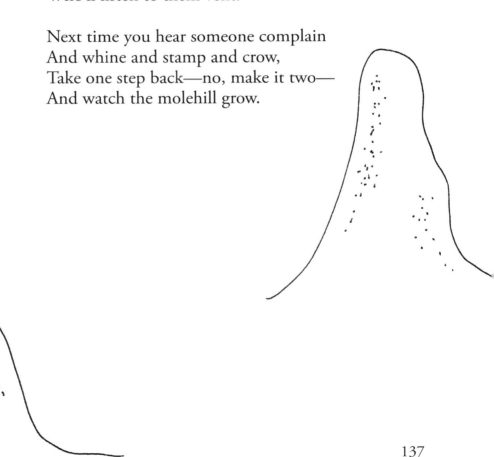

Where do they Go?

Where do the words go
Once they've been said?
Do they bounce from my lips
To the back of your head?

Where do sentences
Dwell once they're through?
For there must be a place
To which they can go, too.

The dreams and ideas
All have a spot
Where they live once they're dreamt
Or rest once they're thought.

The place that they go to
Should have lots of room
For all the new fancies
That come into bloom.

I hope I don't crowd them
With all that I say,
For I dream, talk, and think
Throughout most of the day.

The Perfect
Cup of Cocoa

The perfect cup of cocoa
Is rich and chocolatey,
And always warm, but not too hot—
A steaming chocolate sea.

The surface is enclosed beneath
A thick marshmallow mound,
Which melts into a gooey cloud
Without the slightest sound.

A whipped cream swirl extends beyond
The surface of the cup,
And chocolate sprinkles add
The perfect touch to dress it up.

The perfect cup of cocoa
Is like an old best friend—
It's warm; it's sweet; it's such a treat
And yummy till the end.

Don't Make the Tooth Fairy Angry

"The Tooth Fairy's coming,"
Announced my friend Chase,
Indicating the hole
In the front of his face.

I laughed when he told me;
"How silly!" I said.
"That old gal's a myth,
You big noodle-head."

"You can say what you like,"
He replied solemnly,
"But the Tooth Fairy's real!
Just wait and you'll see!"

"You've been suckered," I said.
"You've been duped. You've been had!"
Thinking Chase was a nice kid,
But not a bright lad.

Yet when I got home,
Beside my toothpaste,
I found a terse note,
Strategically placed:

I slave all night! I work so hard! You simply can't conceive!
The only thing I've asked of you is that you just believe.
But since your disavowal in this morning's little crack,
I've decided you can have your teeth—I want my money back!
So here's a bill for every cuspid, all the molars, too;
I'll have you know that I don't want a dental thing from you!
I'm coming by to get my cash, make no mistake of that.
And if you cannot pay me back, I want your baseball hat!
No Tooth Fairy! I am appalled. How crass! What nerve! What gall!
You'd better have a backup plan to buy that new football!

So the next time somebody
Discredits with zeal,
Tell them, "Think what you want,
But the money is real."

Running Away

I'm running away from home;
I can't take it anymore.
My mom is always telling me
To do just one more chore.

I have to finish homework
Before I watch TV;
If I don't eat all my string beans,
Then it's no dessert for me.

At eight o'clock it's bedtime—
I can't stay up and play—
And I have to keep my room clean
(That's the worst part of my day).

Which is just why I am leaving;
I can't stand to be at home;
I am sure I can do better
If I strike out on my own.

I have almost finished packing
And am just about to go,
But I smell my mother's waffles
(That's my favorite food, you know).

Perhaps my great departure
Could endure a short delay,
As I love my mother's cooking
And it always makes my day.

Mrs. Possum

Dear Mrs. Possum,
Don't you look fine
Wearing your pearls
(Wish they were mine).

But, oh, Mrs. Possum,
They leave you a wreck,
For you don't sleep a wink,
Lest they slip off your neck.

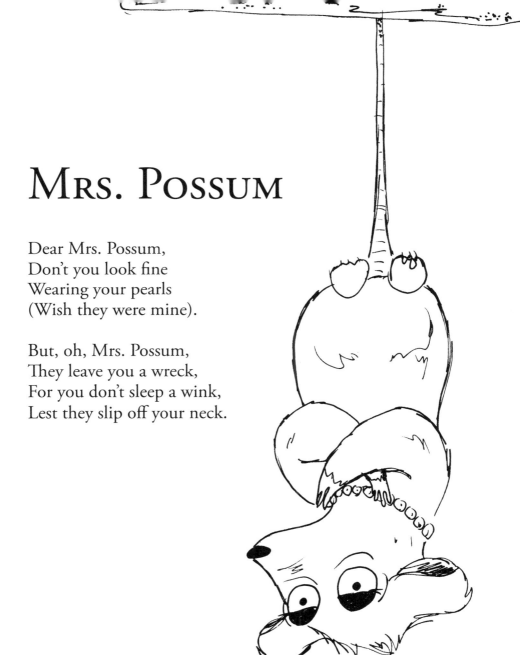

THEY **SHOULD HAVE** LISTENED

They all should have listened to me;
I said spiders for pets were just gross.
But the students all clamored to see them,
And even the teacher got close.

Teddy Drake was so proud of his spiders;
And he laughed at my total chagrin.
Then he pointed and called me a sissy;
Pretty soon the whole class had chimed in.

Hours later when we were all reading,
Peggy Gorman's hand shot in the air.
"Teddy Drake's giant jarful of spiders
Is empty!" she shrieked with despair.

The students all gasped when she said it;
They climbed on their desks as they cried.
So the teacher suggested we line up
And told us we'd have class outside.

As we sat on the cold, windy schoolyard,
All the kids looked at Teddy and glared.
It made me feel quite good to notice
That I wasn't the only one scared.

The next time I say something's icky,
They'll think twice before they disagree.
They'll remember the jarful of spiders,
And then they will listen to me.

NOISY STOMACH

Someone's stomach is growling,
As we take our quiz,
And the whole class is looking
To see whose it is.

We smirk and we smile,
As we look all around;
We search left and right
For the source of the sound.

We whisper the names
Of the ones we suspect,
But it seems the offender
We cannot detect.

So we all shrug our shoulders
And turn to our math;
And I sigh with relief,
Hold my stomach, and laugh.

Happy Chef

I'm a dynamite baker;
Just look at my cake!
'Course it fell in the middle—
A minor mistake.

And sample my cookies;
They're charred but, you'll see,
They still taste like chocolate—
Just slightly crispy.

And please try a muffin;
This recipe's new.
The dough wouldn't rise,
So it's blueberry goo.

It's not how the cooking book
Said it would be,
But it's new and it's better—
Just try and you'll see!

I've unearthed my calling;
It's easy as pie!
You'd just never guess
It's my very first try.

147

Smartest Dog

When I say *sit* my dog lies down;
Rollover makes her bark;
I order her to *fetch the ball,*
But she just roams the park.

When I say *shake* she lifts her ears
And sits up straight and tall,
So proud that she knows what to do
(She's no idea at all).

I tell her *speak*—she stares at me,
Then rolls across the floor;
I order *heel* but she just gapes,
More muddled than before.

Lie down I bid—she lifts her paw
To rest within my palm;
I tell her *come*—she lies in bed
Aloof, detached, and calm.

She barks when I am studying
And comes when I can't play
And rests real quiet on my knee
When I say *go away.*

My dog knows countless other tricks—
It's not that she's not bright—
It's just it takes a time or two
For her to get it right.

Sit, lie down, rollover, shake—
She knows them all quite well;
What matters most is how you ask,
As near as I can tell.

RULES

Rules are irksome;
    Rules are dull,
        And moms know how to make 'em.
That's why we all
    Need grandmas—
        'Cause they're allowed to break 'em.

Sailing

We're setting off
Inside our skiff
To skirr the ocean vast,
To raise the sail
And let the wind
Balloon it from the mast.

We'll chase the waves
And cut them till
They froth a foamy white;
We'll ride the current till
The craggy shore
Is out of sight.

Then when the sun
Is overhead,
Across the deck we'll lie;
And lift our feet
Up in the air
And walk the endless sky.

Bad Luck

Today's the most unlucky day
That I have ever had—
I cannot say I've ever lived
A day that's been this bad.

I dropped a mirror on the floor
And watched it as it burst—
That's seven years of misfortune;
Now I must face the worst.

Then, as I lumbered off to school,
I saw upon the ground
A shiny penny just for me
To turn my luck around.

But, just when all hope was regained,
Disaster reared its head;
I lost the penny I'd retrieved
And found things worse instead.

As if that weren't bad enough,
A black cat crossed my trail;
I'm certain now that test I dread
Is one I'm bound to fail.

I walked beneath a ladder;
My lucky pencil broke—
It's now become extremely clear
My luck's gone up in smoke.

I just can't wait till I go home;
I'm tired of today.
I'll lock myself inside my room
Till this bad luck goes away.

Cannonball

I did a monster cannonball
In the middle of the pool.
I did it to annoy the girls
Out sunning after school.
I did it to show Ben Macay
That I'm a daring man.
I did it for the thrill of it,
And just because I can.
I did it to prove that I'm the kid
Who's good at all the sports.
The only problem seems to be
It made me lose my shorts.

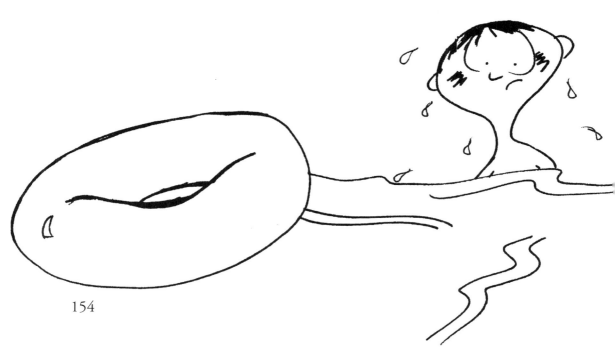

Vacuuming

I'm vacuuming the carpet;
It's quite a dreadful chore.
I don't think I will tell my mom
When I'm bored anymore.

Winter

When the geese are flying south
And the sky is grey, my dears,
Close your eyes and lift your nose;
Listen with your careful ears.

Feel the winter coming on;
Hear it in the crackling trees;
Note the crisping, quivering wind
Sharply snapping at their leaves.

Feel it on the windowpanes—
Chilly glass on fingertips—
Mark the biting of the air,
Heated breath on numbing lips.

See it in the early eves,
In the glowing sunset where
Shadows of the naked trees
Rattle in the biting air.

Watch the nuthatch and the wren;
They know it is time once more
To abandon careful nests,
As they've done each year before.

Let the frost rest on your face;
Sense a shiver on your skin.
See how pretty nature is
When she ushers winter in.

Sand

The sand that goes

Between my toes

Sends tickles way up

To my nose.

Ouch

My arms and legs are black and blue,
A swollen purple mess of goo.
It seems, no matter how I try,
Walls pummel me as I go by.

Weeds

I won't pull up the weeds,
Won't grab them by their heads,
Won't rip their little bodies
From out the flower beds.

How would it make you feel
If someone said to you,
"You are a nasty, ugly thing;
I'm cutting off your view"?

They do not hurt the roses;
Your mums will stay intact.
A weed has feelings, too, you know.
We all do—that's a fact!

I'm standing up for weeds
In gardens coast to coast.
I simply will not pull the weeds—
I'm not that kind of host.

One-Man Band

I play the guitar—
I strum every strand—
While I sing like a bird
In my new one-man band.
I bang on the drums
While my flute pipes along,
Give the cymbals three clangs,
But just one for the gong.
I am the conductor,
The key pianist;
This is clearly the reason
I'm meant to exist.
Who needs other players
With talent this grand?
There's nothing quite like me
And my one-man band.

(But if you're not busy, I'd sure like a hand!)

162

Why Me?

If you have to ask *Why me?*
When you're feeling really blue,
When the world has turned against you
And you don't know what to do,
When it pours colossal raindrops
And the road's a winding mess,
And you're feeling more confused
Than you ever could express,

When the saddened sun won't shine,
When the stars will not align,
When you'd rather be
Inside your bed,
The covers pulled
Above your head,
When life is something
That you dread
And you have to ask *Why me?* . . .

Then when the world seems right and true,
When rain has left a gentle dew,
When you feel happy being you,
Please ask yourself *Why me?* then, too.

Weathergirl Jane

I'm Weathergirl Jane
And I'm here in the rain
To report the forecast
And the weather explain.

In my pink rubber boots,
With a scarf 'round my nose,
I feel quite the pro
In such weathergirl clothes.

I walk 'round the yard
And expound on the state
Of the rain that is here
And the sun we await.

I'm Weathergirl Jane;
My authority's great;
But there's cocoa inside,
And it's time that I ate.

So I'm taking a break
From this dismal, wet gray;
This is Weathergirl Jane
Signing out for the day.

165

Hard Head

The crocodile's a scaly-back;
The armadillo touts his shell.
Myself, I wear a metal hat,
Which suits me just as well.

LIONS

We're lions at the zoo,

And we are telling you

That, **yes, we mind**

Being confined

Three feet from the gnu.

Earful

Don't rush to answer the telephone—
Or be careful if you do—
'Cause it might be Great Aunt Magree,
And then she'll lecture you.

She'll ask about your schoolwork
And all the grades you make,
Then grill you on your spelling
And chastise each mistake.

She'll quiz you on your grammar;
She'll fuss about your speech,
Then rant for five whole minutes
On what the schools should teach.

She'll moan about her aching bones
And describe in great detail
The bunion growing on her toe
That's just below the nail.

And, because she is your aunt,
You cannot just ignore;
Instead you have to listen,
Though it is an awful chore.

So heed the advice that I give you
And, when next your telephone rings,
Just let it keep on sounding—
It's not worth the earache it brings.

Melinda Loved Reading

Melinda loved reading more than she could say
And read from the moment she woke up each day.
Her books were piled high in great stacks by her bed,
For she kept every one that she ever had read.

She read books all day, from the morning till night,
And then in the dark she would read by flashlight.
At dinner she'd sit with a book by her plate,
Pore over the words on the page as she ate.

She'd lie in the attic, a book in her hands,
And dream of the people and far-away lands.
Till one day she opened her book very wide
And leaned too far forward and toppled inside.

She landed amidst all the pictures and words—
Surrounded by adjectives, subjects, and verbs—
Among all the things that kept her entertained;
She liked it in there, and so there she remained.

She now adores traveling from text to text
And darts page to page to see what happens next;
Sometimes if you're reading and very aware,
You'll peer close and notice Melinda in there.

Last Year's Toys

We're last year's toys,
Last year's games,
Season-old dolls
With forgotten names.

It might be nice
To find, somehow,
Another child
Who wants us now.

While old to you,
Our play-days through,
To someone else
We're nice and new.

Whistle, Wind, Down

Whistle, Wind, down;
Turn your breath south;
Push far away
The cold from your mouth.

Whistle, Wind, down
And nudge with your song
The frost and the flurries
That linger too long.

Oh, Wind, if you hear me,
It's time, my dear friend—
For one term's beginning
Is one season's end.

HOLIDAY GREETINGS

I heard you say on Christmas Day,
"Joy! Peace to one and all!"
And 'round the tree you danced with glee
Till from your hair did fall

A ribbon of the deepest red—
A Christmas red, we both averred—
And so we plucked it from the snow
And gave it to a passing bird.

"Oh, thank you! Thank you!" she replied;
"A garland for my nest,
To say today's a special day—
One different from the rest."

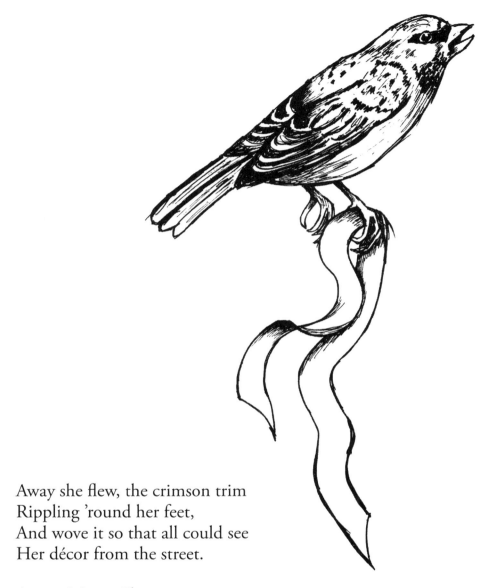

Away she flew, the crimson trim
Rippling 'round her feet,
And wove it so that all could see
Her décor from the street.

A very Merry Christmas to
All birds with snowy berth
Whose voices ring in caroling
Of peace to men on Earth!

It's *Not* a Box

It's *not* a box!
It's an intergalactic
Spaceship fantastic
Jettisoning through the sky.
It's a great pirate ship
Slicing foam at a clip,
The old Jolly Roger up high.
It's a great red balloon,
Loose from its mooring,
Floating on snatches of breeze.
It's a trap! We are captured
By spiteful macaques
Lingering up in the trees.
It's a carpet, a boat,
A bridge o'er a moat,
A steed of a staggering size,
A home for a gnome,
A castle, a cave,
A top-secret car in disguise.
But it's not—
No, it's not—
Nor it was—
Nor it ever will be—
A plain, ordinary,
Just imaginary,
Brown cardboard,
Unrestored,
Most ignored,
Unadored
Box.

Lost Time

Gosh, I'm glad it's Friday—
Two whole days for fun.
Of course, I can't begin to play
Until my schoolwork's done.
And then I have to tidy up
Until my room's just so.
By then I'll likely sigh and ask,
"Where did my weekend go?"

Mail

I'm waiting for the mail to come
And wishing very hard
That someone will have sent to me
A letter or a card.

But generally the mail that comes
Is never in my name.
And, though I keep on hoping,
Things seem to stay the same.

My dad's so lucky—he gets mail
'Most every single day;
The clothing stores and IRS,
They all send things his way.

He's liked so well by his friend Bill
That they write every week;
The more he gets, the more I think
My life seems pretty bleak.

I wish that I got letters
Just half as much as he—
One friend like Bill and I am sure
I'd write back constantly.

I just can't wait till I'm grown up
And folks write me a ton;
Then waiting on the porch for mail
Will be a lot more fun.

Butterflies

I like to sit and watch the sky
And see the butterflies go by;
They flap their wings and ride the breeze,
Then settle down on flowers' leaves.

They do not give the slightest glance
To those who watch their fragile dance,
But flutter on with placid smiles,
Careless of the time and miles.

There's nothing like a lazy day
To sit and dream your cares away.
It makes me smile, and sometimes sigh,
To watch the butterflies go by.

Indexes

Index by Title

Index by First Line